Reindeer and Restraints

A Ménage Romance

Reindeer and Restraints

A Ménage Romance

Part of the
Christmas Cherry Auction series

Sylvie Haas

Copyright

Blurb

My stepbrother is *too* nice... until he reads my spicy romances. Now he's trying a new approach to keep the sexy reindeer wrangler from stealing my heart.

My **older stepbrother** is perfect—sweet, supportive, even lets me live with him rent-free. But his controlled, tidy life doesn't exactly fulfill all of my needs. So I signed up for the **Christmas Cherry Auction**, ready to find my happily ever after.

Then less than a week before the auction, my dreams of a fairytale ending are overtaken by a nightmare. I can still do the auction, but committing to forever is more than I can handle.

Luckily, the **rugged reindeer wrangler** who wins me disagrees. He shows me that freedom can be achieved by giving up control. He'll be my everything if I'll just let my guard down. He's all in, holding the reins and embracing my complicated life.

But it turns out, so is my stepbrother. Suspecting that all of his efforts to win me over are failing, he turns to my spicy romance novels. **Mr. Nice Guy unlocks his naughty side** and tries a new approach to winning me over.

How do I choose when both men are offering me the perfect gift? And is it a problem that my reindeer wrangler didn't exactly tell me who he is?

If you like stepbrothers who unleash their inner beast and will do anything to please their little stepsister, even share her, hand over the reins to the Christmas Cherry Auction!

Chapter 1

Walker

I kneel next to the reindeer trailer, hoping Jeremy has good news on the repairs. There's only an hour left before we need to start loading the animals for the Krampusnacht parade. "Hey, Jeremy, am I going to need to track down a different trailer for tonight?"

He rolls out from underneath. "You're back in business."

"Seriously?" I step back as he stands and wipes his grease-covered hands on his coveralls.

"Call it a Christmas miracle but I tracked down a loose bolt."

"That's it? Thanks for coming out on such short notice. I thought we were screwed."

"Glad to help a friend out."

"I owe you big time. Santa's sleigh can't pull itself. And I sure as hell didn't want to be a no-show for our first Krampusnacht parade here."

Jeremy chuckles, tools clanking as he packs up. "What's the deal with Krampus?"

"Some people are into mythology."

"I don't think that's why my sister's obsessed."

"What do you mean?" I keep my cool exterior. I'm obsessed with his half-sister, Jolene, even though I've only seen pictures of her. Having only been in town a few months, my focus has been on getting the reindeer ranch and children's exploration area established. And since I live on the property, I don't run into many people—exactly how I like it.

"She's been going on and on about getting punished by Krampus."

Now he really has my attention. "Punished?"

"She's a piece of work, got a lot more of our mom's personality than I do." He shakes his head, grabs his tool bags and heads back to his truck. "Always on the lookout for the next adventure. That girl needs to get her head out of the clouds."

She doesn't exactly sound like my type, but it doesn't stop my dick from wanting to give her an adventure. Can I pursue this conversation without freaking my best friend out by letting on that I have a thing for his sister? "What exactly happens at this parade? The Christmas parades I've been to don't involve punishments."

He raises an eyebrow at me and sets his bag in the bed of the truck. "You don't know much about Krampus, do you?"

"Are my reindeer going to be safe?"

He waves off my concern. "They'll be safe, the punishments are all in fun. Krampus hands out bags of coal to the kids, but some of the women, like my sister, enjoy getting spanked or getting tied up and dragged through the parade."

He has no idea what my stoic facade is hiding. If anyone's going to tie up and spank Jolene, it's going to be me.

He continues, "And that's what my sister is hoping for. I think she's read one too many monster romances."

"Monster romance?" I don't have a clue what this is other than the obvious, but do women really fantasize about sex with monsters?

Jeremy straightens, eyebrow arched. "Apparently the idea that women want slow and gentle lovemaking is a little off the mark... at least sometimes, for some women."

I'm too dumbstruck to do anything.

"And on that note, I'll leave you to your preparations." Jeremy opens the driver's door and gets in.

Why did I assume Jolene was sweet and innocent just because she's his little sister? A much bigger question burns, but I don't know how to ask without crossing a line. "Wait, I was wondering about something else."

He laughs. "You mean, your question of the day wasn't about women wanting Santa's dark counterpart to rail them?"

I bite back the growl rising in my throat. If I let on how bad I want to pin Jolene down and make her arch and gasp under me, Jeremy might crawl right back under my trailer and incapacitate it.

Feral doesn't cover how I feel about her. And if she's as adventurous and feisty as he's letting on, she might be bold enough to be in the Christmas Cherry Auction. The thought of her on stage, auctioning off that first time to the highest bidder twists my gut.

Jeremy might know if she's one of this year's virgins.

Focusing my sights on the corral where my reindeer are waiting to be loaded, I stay as casual as I can manage. "Speaking of crazy things that happen in this town, I heard there's a virgin auction."

He hesitates. "More proof to me that I don't understand women. But it's their body, their call, right?"

"Right." Frustration bubbles through me. How do I reconcile that truth with my need to make Jolene mine? "I've heard the women go for millions. How many millionaires are there in this town?"

"Millionaires... billionaires... I can't keep track. The auction's been drawing attention. It's not just guys from here anymore. I don't get it—at least in reality shows like The Bachelor, they go on dates. Or Love is Blind, they talk through walls. Hell, even in Naked Attraction, they strip down, eyeball the goods, and ask a couple questions. Makes more sense than jumping straight to sex for your first hello."

Needing to cover how uncomfortable this is making me, I say, "You'd know compatibility in one department right off the bat."

He shrugs.

I watch the reindeer pace, their breaths visible in the chill. He's not giving any indication Jolene's in it. Am I getting my answer about the possibility of her participating? I think of one last question that should help me tread next to my real question. If he knows she's in it, surely he won't be going. Needing to watch his expression for any hint of discomfort, I face him. "You going to it?"

"Don't make that kind of money turning wrenches. You'd have to spot me a chunk of your inheritance."

I grumble, not entirely sure what I was about to say. There's no way I'd go to the auction with him when the only woman I'd want to win is his sister.

"Just kidding man, I'm not interested. You could check with our brother, Hudson if you want company, but I think he's getting serious about someone, been talking about settling down."

Jeremy had walked me through his family dynamic a while back. I double-check my memory. "Let me get your family straight... You and Jolene have the same mom, right?"

He nods. "Different dads."

"And your mom married a third guy, Hudson's dad?"

"Yeah, but Hudson's just our stepbrother. We don't share any biological parents with him. There's too much going on with steps and halves, we just refer to each other as brothers and sisters. Our family tree is complicated."

I want nothing more than to tangle up in Jolene's world.

Chapter 2

Jolene

My Christmas Cherry Auction dress makes me feel like a celebrity, even with the hem unfinished. I emerge from Starla's bathroom, and the seamstress circles me.

Starla's busy with her eggnog recipe, and Bellamie is focused on the Krampus-themed charm bracelets she's making for a fundraiser.

I throw my arms out to the side and bend a knee, presenting myself. "All right, let's get this thing dialed in. In exactly one week, this dress is going to help me reel in my reverse harem."

The seamstress tugs the fabric around my breasts, her fingers quick and sure. Starla peeks over with her spoon and bowl in hand. "That dress is fire. Those guys will make it rain for you."

Bellamie looks up, both hands on the bracelet she's assembling. "You'll get won for sure. But what if I go on stage and nobody bites?"

I raise a finger to my lips, shushing her from across the room. "It'll work. It always does."

She fidgets with a charm. "How do you find so much confidence?"

"Confidence? Nah, just moving from one adventure to the next."

Starla laughs. "Yeah, like getting spanked by Krampus tonight, then in a week, auctioning your virginity to a pack of billionaires who'll breed you and marry you. Possibly in that order."

"No breeding for me... the implant... remember?"

"How could I forget your auction prep? Get an implant, quit your job, let the auction work its magic."

"Yep, and enjoy my final week of freedom. Well, this type of freedom. Once I snag my harem of billionaires, I'll unlock a whole new kind."

"So what do you actually want tonight? You can't hook up with a Krampus for real?"

"I have no intention of unmasking any of those beasts. The fantasy is all in the costume and the roleplay. I'm the naughty girl. He gets to punish me."

Bellamie shivers. "That's a hard no for me, being tied up and literally paraded in front of everyone."

"Or spanked." I wink at her.

"Worse!"

"Says the one who wants to be bred after the auction. I want time to enjoy my life of luxury. More than a few months with my guys before my body starts getting all..." A shudder runs through me.

Starla says, "Pregnant. It's totally natural."

"I'm not the mothering type yet. Someday I'll have kids... maybe. Should I tell the auction people to announce that as part of winning me—no guarantee of kids. I'm not done figuring out who I am. And who I'll be when I'm loaded? That's the real adventure."

Bellamie says, "I'll need you to be the same rowdy, vivacious friend who drags me into crazy shit."

"I can be the cool aunt."

The dress fitting is going great, making the auction seem so much more real. And then a really freaking hot older dude walks in like he owns the place--straight off a romance novel cover. I hate to admit a ridiculous bias, but he's far too attractive for this to be a home invasion.

But when he strides straight to Starla and pins her against the counter, I'm ready to spring into action. No home invader, no matter how sexy, is going to hurt my friend... except she knows him. Why hasn't she mentioned him?

It's all happening so fast, I can barely process it. Why is she letting him lick drips of eggnog off of her?

I have so many questions. But for now my fitting wraps up, and Starla wants to try her dress on next, no doubt so this guy can see, but we're not supposed to tell anyone we're in the auction ahead of time.

She must know he'll keep quiet.

"What are you wearing, young lady?" Starla's dad's voice bellows from the front door. "I thought you were entering the eggnog contest, not the..." He gestures wildly.

"It's not for tonight." Starla's response gives me a chuckle but fails to address her father's concern.

Her stepbrother, Ryker, walks in behind her dad. Both stare, wide-eyed, but the lust in Ryker's eyes is completely different than the disapproval in her father's.

"Where do you plan on wearing it?" Her dad asks the question she can't answer.

"It's for a Christmas thing."

"Thing?" He won't accept her answer.

She stands a little taller. "It's a Christmas charity auction."

That's dangerously close to— Apparently her dad's heard of it, because he's furious. She spills the whole deal, arguing with her dad and brother about appropriateness, but it's the other guy's reaction, the one who was licking eggnog off of her, that really surprises me.

He says, "There's no way my best friend's daughter is going to sell her virginity."

Surely she would have told us if she had a thing with him. Now is not the time to focus on that. Her dad grounded her from going to the auction. Who grounds their twenty-two-year-old daughter?

The rest of the dress fitting is marred by the argument. I bet this is more than the seamstress bargained for.

I wait until we're in the car on the way to the Krampusnacht festival to help Starla brainstorm how to sneak out so she can get to the auction. And even though she swears there's nothing between her and her dad's best friend, Bellamie and I are certain he'd like to change that.

Too bad he missed his chance. As of Friday, we'll all have new lives with the guys who win us in the auction.

The parade kicks off, and I scream so loud I scare the little girl next to us when the Krampuses come into sight—towering figures of fur, curling horns, and rusty sleigh bells clanging on chains. They stalk the route, growling at onlookers, tossing little burlap sacks labeled "COAL" to squealing children.

Waving wildly, I vie for their attention. One Krampus locks eyes with me—or so I think. It's hard to tell with the mask. He stomps toward our spot on the curb.

Excitement surges.

He veers at the last second, zeroing in on Bellamie. He's choosing her. No! It's all wrong. She doesn't want this.

But when he turns her around so he can spank her, I catch a glint of something in her eyes. She finally gets it—the fantasy.

Krampus grabs her wrists, draping a leather binding over them, pausing, and giving her a chance to back out. I can't breathe, I'm so ecstatic that she gets this opportunity. Will she take it?

I don't even care if I get a Krampus. It would mean so much more to me for her to break free from her good girl persona and see how exciting life can be.

Krampus works the leather around her wrists, tugs the binding, and pulls her into the parade. I'm losing my mind, once again causing the little girl next to us to stand closer to her mother. More proof I'm not ready for kids.

I try to grab the attention of other Krampuses parading past us, but tonight's not my lucky night.

The dark clanging of Krampus chains and old sleigh bells gives way to joyful bells and reindeer pulling Santa's sleigh, marking the end of my chance for a Krampus.

It can hardly be a bad night when I get to see real live reindeer. They're pretty amazing.

And if I have to bank my luck, I'll save it for the auction.

The reindeer and sleigh pass, allowing my sights to land on a burly, rugged, sexy AF dude in a flannel shirt and overalls. My heart sends out new fireworks. Who needs Krampus, when this guy exists?

Our eyes meet, and I'm certain of it this time because there's no mask in the way. My ovaries beg me to get rid of the implant. I've never felt like this before.

Then he abruptly looks down. I follow his gaze. He stepped in reindeer poop. Yuck.

Only then do I notice the shovel and wheelbarrow he's toting. He gets to work cleaning the street.

Starla grabs my arm. "We have to find Bellamie."

She's not wrong. And I'd be foolish to jeopardize my chances at the auction by falling for a poop scooper. But still... there's something about him.

If the auction doesn't work out, like last year when the virgins weren't able to make it because of a blizzard, I can track this guy down. It can't be that hard to find out who provided cleanup for the reindeer at the parade.

Chapter 3

Jolene

Starla's table looks like a craft store explosion, with every color of sequins, beads, and felt for the Christmas stockings she needs help making. Bellamie, me, and another friend, Penny, all showed up to help her finish her commitment to the foster care agency.

I have my suspicions about why she didn't finish them last night, but bide my time asking. Krampus asked her out, and I think she went.

I sew a line of gold beads onto the harness around the felt reindeer's neck then pass it to Penny. My mind still buzzes from the parade. The reindeer wrangler fantasy lingers in my thoughts. It rivals for space with my stepbrother fantasy. We're all more than a little obsessed with our stepbrothers.

They'd assumed I had the best chance of hooking up with mine, since Hudson invited me to live with him and he pays all of the bills. But we're still in separate bedrooms.

"Either of you think your stepbrothers will show up at the auction?"

No luck for any of us. Starla sews silver beads onto a felt snowflake. "I checked the weather and it's not supposed to snow Friday."

I whoop. "Good thing. I'd lose my mind if we got snowed out like the virgins from last year."

"I can't believe the waitresses stepped up to help. That would be too much for me." Penny attaches the reindeer I passed to her onto a felt stocking.

She's pretty reserved, but I thought the allure of a luxurious future might win her over.

Bellamie asks her, "Do you regret turning the invitation down, Penny?"

Penny pauses her sewing. We give her a second. "I don't know how they chose who to send invitations to. Why me? I've thought about it so many times–how simple it should be to get on stage, let the men bid, and find a happily ever after."

"I bet you could still do it." I grab my phone, ready to see if we can get her in.

Penny moves her hands to her lap. "I said it would be simple, not easy. I get anxious just thinking about stepping on stage, presenting myself to the bidders."

Her breathing heightens, and Bellamie rubs her shoulder. "It's okay, Penny. No one will force you."

I smile warmly as Bellamie says. "She's right, Penny, there's no pressure for you to participate in the auction if you don't want to. But—"

A buzz from my phone draws my attention. I tap the screen to dismiss my brother Jeremy's message and continue playfully. "But, I think it's time we force Bellamie to tell us why she couldn't finish these stockings last night."

Bellamie sets her sewing down and steeples her fingers in front of her mouth. "I took your advice and went out with Krampus."

"You did?!" My surprise bubbles out.

She gives us enough details that it's clear we've unleashed a beast. She thinks they're soulmates or something and isn't sure she'll do the auction.

"Excellent backup plan. Not that you'll need one." I'm sure we'll all be fine at the auction, but if not, she has Krampus, and I have a poop scooper.

This auction really needs to work.

Another text message alert draws my attention. My heart stops. My phone instantly rings. "I need to take this."

I rush outside, needing space to absorb the message that my cousin passed away.

I answer Jeremy's call when I can breathe in the cool air, relieving the feeling of suffocation. "Is this some sick—"

"It's not. And there's no easy way to put this. She named you as guardian of Jane."

15

"What?" My chest tightens and I'm not sure if the word makes it out of my mouth or not.

"You're now the mother of a two-year-old."

"Why me?" Why not Jeremy? Why not any other relative? Can I say no? I'm sweating despite the cold air.

"I don't know. Trust me, I'm shocked too."

Jeremy's comment isn't even offensive. Everyone knows I'm not mom material. We wrap up the call and I breathe deeply, sucking in gulps of air a few more times, waiting to wake up. I don't.

Returning to my friends, I say, "I have to leave."

"What's wrong?" Bellamie asks.

They all get up from the table and help me get my things.

"Am I cursed?" I ask, feeling selfish that I can even think about myself right now.

"What do you mean?"

"I can't do the auction."

"Why?"

"I've just been named guardian of my cousin's two-year-old daughter."

Silence fills the room before I share the tragic details of my cousin's car wreck. She was a single mom and had the foresight to name a guardian—me.

Starla turns to Penny. "I'm betting you don't want to take Jolene's place either?"

16

Did somebody ask Penny to take their place in the auction? Is Bellamie that serious about Krampus?

Penny shakes her head. "I'm sorry, I can't. But Jolene can still do the auction."

My shoulders slump. "I have a kid now. Don't get me wrong. I love her."

Penny's tone is calm. "You're still a virgin."

"Who would want to bid on a mom?" Reality drops on me in clumps. "Oh my god. I'd have to hire a babysitter."

Bellamie's phone rings but she finishes the call quickly and brings me a tissue. "Time to make a game plan for Mama Jo."

I think I hate the nickname.

Bellamie's quick to offer, "I can whip up some casseroles for your freezer and coordinate meals so that you don't have to do any cooking while you transition into motherhood. And I'll definitely help with babysitting, because I'm guessing you're going to have to get some affairs in order."

Starla offers to help too. Penny says," I'll cook meals for you and I can run errands, but don't ask me to babysit."

"I have the best friends." Despite my words, for the first time ever, I struggle to feel joy.

Bellamie says, "You don't have to go into motherhood alone. We're here for you. And if I can remain a virgin by turning down sex with the hottest, most perfect guy I've ever met, we can certainly find you a babysitter for Friday night."

"Hudson will lose it if I spring a two-year-old on him. He's so tidy. I think he already realized he made a mistake by inviting me to live with him."

"He adores you," Starla assures me.

"He *did*, but he's been dropping hints about settling down, futures, and commitments. I haven't been able to figure out if he's trying to tell me he has a girlfriend, or that I need to get a life." I squeeze my eyes shut. "Either way, I can't be a third wheel with a kid, cluttering his world."

"Take a breath," Bellamie says calmly.

"I quit my job." The words tumble out.

Starla scoots closer, her knee bumping mine. "They'll take you back at the coffee shop. They loved you."

I shake my head. "It's barely enough to support me, much less a toddler? Oh my god, what about college? I need to start saving up for that. I see the error of my—"

"Calm down," Starla gives me a hug. "No need to worry about college yet. Do you think your cousin had life insurance?"

"Not a chance. She jumped from one dead-end job to another."

Bellamie asks, "What about the baby's father?"

"She wasn't sure who it was, but said she'd told the most likely candidate. He ghosted her. Not the type of person you want in a kid's life. Jane needs stability."

Bellamie squeezes my shoulder. "Look at you going into mom mode already."

I cringe. Did she not hear me say that Jane needs stability? How am I supposed to provide that?

Starla reframes their earlier support. "You might be the cool aunt to our kids someday, but we'll be the doting aunts to yours now."

Bellamie gives wholehearted agreement.

A dark laugh bubbles up. "What if I screw up? What if I break her?"

"You won't," Starla assures me.

The shock subsides enough that tears threaten. I blink them back. "I need to tell Hudson."

I type out a text to him: *We need to talk right away.*

"Want us to tag along?"

"Thanks, but I need to do this alone."

Starla says, "We're a call away—day, night, meltdown o'clock. Backup squad activated."

Warmth spreads through my chest, easing the edge of the fear. This isn't the adventure I'd hoped for.

Chapter 4

Hudson

I crease the end of the wrapping paper into a triangle, making sure both sides are equal. Tugging it tightly against the side of the package, I apply a single strip of invisible tape—such a misnomer. It's clearly there, but at least it's less noticeable than other tape.

Jolene's been dodging my hints for weeks, but I've laid them out like blueprints: lingering glances over her favorite foods that I prepared, comments about her future, even a conversation about whether she wants kids.

Am I being too subtle? Am I not serious enough? Is she fearful of commitment because of how complicated our family feels sometimes? Marriage means something solid to me, an anchor against the maelstrom. I want to spend the rest of my life devoted to Jolene.

Or is she just being Jolene, freaked out by anything that will pin her down and end her adventures as she calls life?

This gift will change everything—a marriage proposal that she can hold in her hands, no chance for a misunderstanding. And I'll be able to explain that I'll take care of the things that bog her down like bills. She'll have guaranteed freedom... and me.

I carry the package to the tree and set it underneath. Back at the table, my phone buzzes. I hurry over to find Jolene's name on the screen. My heart skips a beat. Does she somehow know what I'm doing? Is she spying on me?

I glance over my shoulder even though I'm certain she's not home. She made a big deal about how excited she was that Bellamie asked for help with one of her charity projects.

Knowing that she'd be gone for several hours gave me the perfect opportunity to lay the engagement plan out on the table, survey it for accuracy one last time, then wrap it for a Christmas surprise.

Convinced she's not lurking, I swipe open the text.

Jolene: *Super serious. We need to talk. On my way home*

Me: *Call me*

Jolene: *Has to be in person.*

Maybe she caught the hints after all. Her friends probably nudged her—I've overheard their chatter filtering through walls, giggles about stepbrothers.

I manage a thumbs-up emoji before sending the phone clattering to the table. I snatch it up, check the screen. Fine, of course, with my Otter Box case.

This is it. I stride to the tree, nudge the box front and center. If she seems ready and even remotely acknowledges my hints, I'll give this to her today.

No more pretending we're just roommates playing house. No restraining myself at night when she masturbates far too loudly. I can be the reason for her moans.

She has to sense why I begged her to move in, why I foot every bill, scrub counters after her midnight snacks, and plate dinners like we're at a five-star restaurant.

Jolene: *Be home in 20 minutes*

Another thumbs-up. Then inspiration strikes.

I grab the log of her favorite cookie dough that I stashed in the back of the fridge, then crank the oven to 350. I cut carefully, making sure not to squish the star shape that's in the middle of the dough.

The scent of fresh-baked cookies will set the tone the second she walks in the door.

In the nine minutes those need to bake, I bolt to the bathroom and shower as fast as possible, lathering up with Old Spice *Kraken*, another one of her favorites. I don't know if she actually likes the scent or is fascinated by the Kraken like she is with her monster romances.

Rinse, towel-dry, and I'm done in minutes. I yank on the light-blue Henley that she says brings out my ocean-blue eyes, and add my pair of new jeans. And since barefoot seems too casual for the day that will change the rest of my life, I add my Dude sliders.

The timer dings, and I rush back to the kitchen. Lightly golden edges and a bright star in the center look perfect. I pull the tray out and set it on a cooling rack.

Keys jangle at the door. She's here.

I wipe my palms on a kitchen towel and force myself to breathe. Whatever she says, I end this charade today. No more hints. Just truth.

I make a mental note of the time so I can remove the cookies from the pan in three minutes. But if our conversation goes long like I hope, imperfect cookies won't be a problem.

The door flies open, and Jolene bursts in, cheeks flushed, eyes wild.

Shock washes through me. I reposition my feet and fling the oven mitt onto the counter. She was supposed to be happy.

The gift box under the tree taunts me. Would it fix the problem or make it worse?

I rush forward and pull her into my arms. She stiffens for a split second, then sags against me. I kick the door shut.

We stand there, my chin resting on her head. Her citrusy shampoo mixes with the sugar wafting from the oven, such a sweet combination at odds with the chaos on her shoulders. But she wants to talk, she's trusting me to help.

That's what I'll do—put my agenda aside and tend to hers. I ease back, set my hands on her shoulders. Her green eyes shimmer, red-rimmed, searching mine like she's already defeated.

"Let's go to the couch," I say. "I'll grab cookies and milk."

She sniffles. "You always know how to make me happy, but this is bigger than cookies and milk."

The flatness of her tone fills me with worry. Whoever hurt her is going to pay.

She slips from my grip, paces to the living room, and sinks into the couch cushions.

"What's going on, Jolene? I'll fix it."

"You can't." She twists her fingers in her lap and stares at the floor. "I'll get a job. I'll figure this out."

"What are you going to fix with a job?" My pulse thuds heavily in my veins.

"My cousin..." She lifts her gaze and her voice cracks. "Jennifer died in a car wreck and named me as guardian of Jane. I don't know what to do with a two-year-old!"

My mouth goes slack as I struggle to know what to say. Jennifer was just getting her life under control—for Jane—and now she's gone. Why would she name Jolene as guardian? They weren't that close. And not to make light of the tragedy, but Jolene has made it clear many times that she's not mom material. Her despair makes sense.

"Hey." I reach for her. "You don't have to tackle this solo. I'll help."

She shakes her head. "I won't dump a kid on you. That's not right."

"Taking care of a child who just lost their mom is right. She'll fit into our little world." The words tumble, rawness almost revealing my bigger plans. "I want to raise her with you."

Her eyes widen. "You're not kicking me out?"

"Why would I kick you out? I want to—"

She cuts me off, voice firm. "Don't make any promises you'll regret."

"I won't regret helping. How about we take it a month at a time. Promise you won't make any big decisions without talking to me?"

She exhales shakily. "You're my shelter in the storm."

"Where is Jane now? When do we pick her up?"

"Social Services is gathering her things, then they'll be on their way."

Her breathing evens against my side. I squeeze my arm over her shoulders and pull her close. I can feel how fragile she is right now. The proposal will have to wait.

But the milk and cookies won't. "I'll get a snack, then clear a bedroom for her."

Chapter 5

Jolene

Bellamie wheels the cart down the baby aisle, her laughter bubbling up as Jane plays with a toy attached to the handle.

Jane's fingers are so tiny—not abnormally small, they fit her hands nicely, but everything about her is small... and needy. She doesn't know what's safe or not, and judging by the variety of things she's explored with her mouth, she needs someone wise to care for her. She needs someone like Bellamie who thought to bring a wipe to clean the cart.

She got me. What was my cousin thinking?

Starla flanks me on the other side, her arm looped through mine, as we study shelves stacked with gadgets I never imagined needing. Monitors that beam live feeds to your phone. Lamps that play nature sounds and change colors. Plush toys that hum lullabies. Do they make these in adult sizes? I could use a stuffed animal that would drown out the panic.

How did we survive as humans before all of this was invented?

Bellamie halts at the diaper display, a wall of plastic packages and boxes each touting some spectacular capability. She tilts her head, scanning the options. "These match what she came with, so we don't have to worry about an allergic reaction."

"To a diaper?" My question is mostly rhetorical, but the buzz of my phone draws my attention.

It's Jeremy, and I feel bad that some selfish, desperate part of me hopes he was able to track down Jane's father.

I let Bellamie and Starla know I need to take the call.

"Any luck?" I ask as soon as I answer.

Jeremy doesn't even give me shit. He just says, "I wish I had better news."

Relief floods me. The unexpected reaction leaves me speechless. Why am I relieved?

"Jolene? You okay?"

"Yeah, actually, I am."

We hang up, and as I walk back to the cart, Jane smiles and babbles at me. I don't have any idea what she says, or how long it will take me to feel like a mom, but it's time I grow up.

Hudson had no idea how helpful all of his recent questions would be. He planted the seed in my mind that I'm not a teenager anymore and I'm going to have to pivot when things don't go as planned.

Being gifted a child definitely wasn't my plan. I glance at Bellamie and Starla, their faces expectant. Lucky doesn't cover having them here, helping me through this.

"Everything okay?" Starla asks.

I pocket the phone. "Yeah. Jeremy couldn't find Jane's dad. So it's official. I'm doing this."

Starla's arms wrap around me. "Jane's lucky to have you."

"Lucky might be a stretch. I don't know what I'd do without you two."

Bellamie grins, pushing the cart forward. "You'd manage. But hey, did you talk to Laz about the auction?"

I nod, my pulse quickening at the thought of going through with it. "Yeah. I still qualify. The contract doesn't say we can't have kids, so we're considering whether we reveal that tidbit when I take the stage."

"I'm so excited." Starla pumps a fist. "It wouldn't have been right without you."

My phone dings again. Jeremy sent a link for a reindeer ranch followed by: *They have stuff for kids to do. Check it out. Jane might like it.*

How does Jeremy know about this? And is this something a toddler would like? Jane can't possibly understand what a reindeer is. But it's probably better than sitting at home.

"Have you heard of the reindeer ranch?" I ask my friends.

Bellamie lights up. "Yeah, it's new. They provided the reindeer for the Krampusnacht parade."

Is this what mom brain is like? I can't even remember that I saw reindeer and *him* a few days ago. I can't believe I'd forgotten the poop scooper. How many days was it? Less than a week? Whew, so much has happened.

Starla plucks a plush reindeer from the endcap and wiggles it in front of Jane's face, making her squeal in delight.

Then her tiny fingers grab the toy and plunge it straight into her mouth.

I'm close to gagging, thinking how many people have touched it. I make a mental note to pack lots of extra wipes when we go to the ranch—and not to let her get her mouth on any real reindeer.

"I'd love to go to the ranch with you, but my schedule's pretty full. I'll find someone to go with you, though," Bellamie says.

"You don't have to do that."

"I want to. I have to make sure you survive so you make it to the auction."

"In that case, thank you. I need the auction more than ever, even if it just turns into one night of fun."

Chapter 6

Walker

I grip the rough cedar post harder than necessary, my knuckles whitening against the hard wood. While I pretend to be checking the joints, my gaze locks on the woman across the corral.

Her blonde hair sparkles, literally, in the winter sun. She seems to have tinsel in her hair. She looks so familiar, but I don't know anyone who wears tinsel.

Her expression hints at a struggle beneath her happy exterior. She balances a squirming toddler on her hip—sufficient enough reason for a struggle.

Something primal stirs in my chest—protectiveness, the need to claim her, the desire to make her mine. Whatever her struggle, I need to fix it.

She's here with a girlfriend, not a husband or boyfriend, and I already confirmed there's no ring on her finger. Is the baby daddy a deadbeat?

I force my gaze to the parent tending to a kid who's having a meltdown. I don't have the patience for that. Why am I letting my dick get hard over a mom?

Fuck, I don't even know if she's available. Why can't I shake this need to be with her?

Her gaze fixes on me, and I hold it for a moment, then nod. Adrenaline races through me. Did she stare because I was staring or because we have something?

I step into the corral and run my hand over one of the reindeer's backs, making sure I look official. I'd continue across the corral in a heartbeat if she didn't have a kid. My mind flashes to pinning her against the barn wall, her breath hitching as I slide my hand up her thigh. But I'm the ranch owner, not some rutting buck.

The toddler points at the reindeer, her giggles slicing through the crisp air. The blonde leans in, murmuring something that draws a brighter squeal from the kid.

"Thanks for coming, Molly. I had to get out with this little one, and Bellamie and Starla were busy. Have you ever been to a reindeer farm?" The blonde's voice carries. "Did you even know they existed?"

Molly hesitates, eyes flicking to the antlered animals milling in the enclosure. Reindeer snort and paw the ground. Molly seems to be studying them before she says, "There's a first time for everything. Life's just one big adventure, right?"

Interesting. She didn't answer either question.

The blonde laughs, a hint of sadness weighing it down. "Yeah, adventure. That's how I've always rolled. Until this little one." She holds the toddler up as if taking a better look. She returns the kid to her hip, and they both peer over the fence.

A sharp scream erupts from beside them—a different kid, red-faced and wailing as a reindeer nudges too close.

"I'm so glad Jane's not afraid of reindeer. Not sure I'm ready for a meltdown." Blondie sounds grateful, but surely she's managed meltdowns before. She ushers the comment away by pressing a big, fat kiss to Jane's chubby cheek.

I'm decidedly a selfish prick for wanting to give her something else to plant a big, fat kiss on. Yet, I move one fence panel closer.

Brighter than before, she says, "One perk of having a kid is that I get to do all these fun things I would've skipped otherwise."

Molly ponders the statement and seems almost longing. "Yeah, a kid opens up activities that would seem weird solo."

The blonde tilts her head. "Want to hold her?"

Molly pauses longer than the question deserves. Most people have a pretty clear idea if they want to hold a kid or not. I'm a no—unless Blondie asks me to. Then I'd figure it out.

"I'm not really sure how," Molly admits. That makes a little more sense.

The blonde cups a hand over Jane's ear and stage-whispers. "I didn't even want kids. Do you?"

Molly seems caught off guard. "How can you really know for sure?"

And we're back to the not-so-straightforward answers.

Blondie holds the kid toward Molly, who hesitantly accepts her. Even though she indicated she's not familiar with holding kids, they fit together seamlessly.

"If you'd gotten an invite to the auction, would you have gone the standard route of starting a family right away?" Curiosity laces Blondie's odd question.

The question's so unexpected, I have to replay the words in my mind.

Molly shrugs, smiling warmly at Jane. "Hard to say since I didn't get one."

"Surely you thought about it. For me it was the happily ever after but not the babies. And of course, it's super cool that the Christmas Cherry Auction gives us a way to *use* our virginity."

Christmas Cherry Auction. The words slam into me. My throat tightens. I cough hard, doubling over, resting my forearms on the top rail.

Blondie's in the auction—she has to be a virgin. Was I wrong to think Jane was her kid?

Crap, Blondie's looking at me like I'm contagious. I rush to one of the water stations as if something got caught in my throat. In my periphery, I track them. They move to the barn that houses the children's exhibits.

That's a place I rarely set foot in, even at our first location. I hire someone to hang out near the kids. But as the owner, I won't get questioned for spending a little time there.

Blondie, Molly, and Jane stop at the Make It Rein exhibit. Wooden reindeer pull a pint-sized Santa sleigh the kids can sit in. The wall contains an exhibit of different types of reins.

Jane climbs into the sleigh seat, her giggles bubbling as Molly hands her the reins. The kid flaps them wildly.

"Will you stay with her?" Blondie asks Molly. "I want to snap a picture."

"Absolutely. You sure you don't want me to take it so you can be with Jane?"

"Not ready to see myself in full mom mode yet."

Hmmm.

Blondie steps backward while watching her phone screen. She's more focused on getting the right shot than her surroundings. She doesn't notice the kid running toward her.

I rush forward to intervene. I'm pretty sure my movement causes her to glance sideways and notice the kid.

Carefully swiping the kid to safety, I'm one step too far away to stop Blondie from stumbling. Her arms windmill. Her diaper bag swings. And she crashes into the wall.

It's sturdy enough to withstand the impact, but multiple reins fall free. They're designed to be interacted with, but not quite like this.

As she scrambles to contain herself, she inadvertently tangles with the various reins. It's like watching the sexiest trainwreck of all time.

My hands find her first—fingers closing firmly around her tiny waist and all of the errant straps. The intimate touch combined with the leather hits me in a way I haven't felt before.

Steadying her, I move my hands to her shoulders. "Stop moving," I growl. "I'll untangle you."

She freezes, breath catching. I worry that I sounded angry, but her eyes lift to mine—green, wide and unflinching.

That moment we shared from across the corral is nothing compared to this. My cock lengthens against my thigh—getting hard in the children's barn is more proof that I'm not cut out for being a parent, but I want nothing more than to put a baby in this woman.

"Are you okay?" Molly calls out from the sleigh.

We both answer yes and I get to work pulling the reins from her. How the hell did she wrap three loops around one wrist? I stroke my thumb over the inside of her wrist. Is she into this kind of thing... in the bedroom, not in the children's barn.

"Thank God I wasn't holding Jane," she says, half-laugh, half-groan.

Sliding the last rein over her shoulder, I'm unable to step away. I fail to do anything but stare. I force out, "You sure you're okay?"

"I'm fine. Bet no one's ever done that before." She returns the strap of the diaper bag to her shoulder. "I'm pretty special."

"Yes, you are." I grab her hands again, not really sure why. The air electrifies. Her sweet vanilla scent floods my senses. I could pull her closer, see if she tastes—what the fuck is wrong with me?

She glances down at our hands, then back up. We just stand there, lost in the moment. I should ask her out. I have to stop her from going to the auction.

Jane's fuss kills the mood. Molly carries the squirmy kid closer, a ripe, unmistakable whiff in the air. Sweet vanilla gone.

"Ewww." Blondie slips free, grabbing Jane. "Gotta handle this."

"Bathroom's that way." I point down the hall and watch her go.

Molly helps rehang one of the reins that fell to the ground. "She's new to this."

"To crashing displays?" I grunt, smoothing my fingers over a leather strap to mask the pounding in my chest.

Molly laughs. "To being a mom." Molly glances toward the door. "Wouldn't even know this place had a kid exhibit if her brother hadn't tipped her off."

Seizing my chance to get more information about Blondie, I ask, "Does he work here?"

"Kind of. He's a mechanic. Comes when needed."

"Jeremy?"

36

"Yeah."

The pieces slot together. This is Jolene. She looks a lot different than the picture I saw of her, different hair color and without makeup. But now I see it. That's why I'm so drawn to her. She's the forbidden woman I've been craving.

I can't ask her out, Jeremy would kill me. But if I win her, I'll have a contractual obligation to claim her. Jeremy wouldn't have the heart to kill his sister's baby daddy.

She emerges minutes later with Jane fresh and happy. "That was the last diaper, we better go."

Molly falls in step, and they head toward the exit. I trail at a distance, mind racing. The auction's in two days.

Rushing to my office, I pull out my phone so I can educate myself about this auction. There's no room for error. She's mine to claim.

Chapter 7

Jolene

Walking into the dressing room at the Aubergine Affair, a chuckle escapes me, drawing Bellamie and Starla's attention. I mutter, "I'm really here." Then I raise my voice, "I'm so glad we all made it to the auction."

Bellamie, Starla, and I share a moment of excitement, then start getting ready.

Helping Bellamie zip up her auction dress, I say, "Thank you so much for finding a babysitter for me."

"We wouldn't have accepted the invitations without your encouragement. The least I could do was make sure you got your turn on—oh my gosh, I almost forgot the goodie bags I made."

"You didn't have to do that, Bellamie," Starla says.

Grabbing the small, red organza bags from her purse, Bellamie sets the special one for Jefferson, the emcee, to the side and hands the others to Starla and me. "I wanted to. They're survival kits, really, full of blister Band-Aids, an assortment of headache pills, gum, safety pins–those sorts of things."

"Thank you," we say at the same time.

I'm checking out the goodies she included in our bags when my phone rings. "Oh no, it's the babysitter." Did I celebrate being here too soon?

"Whatever it is, we'll figure it out," Bellamie assures me.

The ringing continues. I can't make myself take the call.

"Want me to get it for you?" Bellamie asks.

"Yes, I'm such a terrible mom. I just want one evening to myself."

Starla laughs. "You sound like a seasoned mother already."

Bellamie takes the call, easily sorting out where Jane's woobie might be. "It's in my car. She's on her way to pick it up."

"Sacred blankets, so much to keep track of. What would I do without you?"

"You wouldn't lose woobies in my backseat."

A knock on the dressing room door is followed by Laz, the owner of the Aubergine Affair, asking, "Can I come in? I have some exciting news to share."

Starla tugs her dress up. "Yep, we're all decent."

"Great news, ladies!" He enters and flashes the program at us.

Bellamie takes the shiny cardstock from him and gasps.

"Hot off the presses. Molly is on her way, and Roxy is bringing a dress that should fit her."

The three of us are too confused or stunned to react. Roxy was in the first Christmas Cherry Auction and still lives in the area. She's friends with everyone so it doesn't surprise me she could find a dress for Molly at a moment's notice.

"That's what you wanted, right?" Laz asks.

Starla and I jump up and down, squealing in excitement.

"Oh my gosh, really?" The ponderous tone in Bellamie's voice makes me worry that she can't get Krampus off her mind and is looking for a way out of the auction. I'd almost forgotten about her situation.

"Yeah, after you contacted us, we looked into it and long story short, her invite must have gotten lost."

While he continues, I'm watching Bellamie's wheels turn. We can't let her back out. Being in the auction is a once-in-a-lifetime opportunity.

"Does this mean she can take my place?" Bellamie's question verifies my concern.

"She's not taking anyone's place. We added her." Laz tips the edge of the program down so he can point to the names.

I have to convince her to stay. I step close. "Don't back out."

Laz is confused. "Yeah, don't back out. We're reprinting the programs. This was the first one, I grabbed it off the copier to show you because I thought you'd be excited."

"We are," I say.

"Bellamie?" Laz asks.

"Can I have a minute?"

40

"If you're backing out, we'll have to reprint. I need to know right away." He checks his phone.

Starla ushers him out of the room, then she and I team up on Bellamie, determined to support her the way she supports us.

"What if this is a sign?" Bellamie asks.

A sign. That gives me an idea. I take the program from her and hold it up. "It is a sign. Read it."

She stares blankly so I start at the top, pointing to my name. "Jolene, that's me."

Pointing to Starla, I read her name. Then sliding my finger back and forth under Bellamie's name, I state slowly, "Bellamie, that's you."

"I know, but–"

"And then, Molly." I move my finger down. "There are four of us now. It's a sign. You helped make sure she was included, the same way as you made sure I was. Now we're going to return the favor."

When she doesn't shake free from her indecision, Starla says, "Dating's a crapshoot, Bellamie. You don't even know if Krampus will show up on Sunday."

"Or why he won't tell you his name." I step toward the door, ready to wrap this up the second she shows a sign of agreement.

Starla gives her a hug. "Ready to give the auction a chance?"

"Yes." Bellamie's answer is weak, but sufficient.

"She's in, Laz," I call through the open door.

"Oh shoot." Bellamie snaps back to life. "I have to meet the babysitter for the woobie handoff."

I'm so grateful for a friend like her, and only have a tiny bit of worry that she'll use the woobie handoff as a chance to sneak away.

Laz comes in after Bellamie exits. "One last detail. Have you decided on whether to announce that you have a kid or not?"

"Let's do it—save me from having an awkward conversation afterward."

"You're sure? Some men—"

"At this point, all I'm counting on is the auction setting me up for a mind-blowing first sexual experience. I just got a lifelong commitment thrust on me. I don't want to push that on anyone else who's not ready."

"Good point." Starla touches up her lipstick. "Skip right to the guys who will accept a stepdaughter as part of a happily ever after."

Smiling warmly at her, I add, "And avoid a mood-killing conversation."

Laz rubs his chin. "One solid bidder, that's all it takes."

Does he not understand the allure of a reverse harem? "Right."

Molly shows up, and Laz leaves us alone to get her ready.

Before long, my name is being called from the stage. I take my place under the lights. All I can think about is that I belong here. It's my time to shine.

The crowd hushes, a sea of eager bidders listening intently as Jefferson introduces me.

My reality comes crashing back down with the mention of me having a two-year-old. It was the right choice to have it declared up front. Thankfully, the smattering of applause and catcalls boosts my confidence that I'll get bid on.

Jefferson continues, "I'm going to turn this over to the auctioneer, and let's see who starts the bidding."

Letting my true spirit shine, I strut across the stage, channeling every ounce of my adventurous vibe, even if I now pack sippy cups for my adventures.

Bids take off. "Fifty thousand... one hundred!" My heart soars. I'm lost in the rush, the dream unfolding, eyes drifting over the crowd without landing. Numbers blur—half a mil? A million? Doesn't matter. This is my spotlight.

As the dollar amounts continue upward, the number of bidders drops. One of the remaining bidders is in the front. His crisp shirt, perfectly styled hair, and controlled smile are too buttoned-up for my flair, but I won't judge. He exudes stability... and solid dad potential. As do his friends who appear to be in on this with him.

But is he, or are they, right for me?

Gibberish tumbles from the auctioneer's mouth, and a new bidder number joins the fun.

I scan the room to see who was holding out. In the back of the room, the poop scooper... or maybe I should call him the reindeer wrangler is holding up a bidder's paddle.

Broad shoulders fill out his flannel shirt. His stoic expression serves as a reminder of how annoyed he looked when I messed up the display. Why is he bidding on me?

Yes, I thought we shared something, but that was heavily impacted by how my body reacted to his strong hands circling my waist and the way his rugged jawline made me swoon. And the reins... the brief moment when I swore he rubbed his thumb over the inside of my wrist as if he was having thoughts of binding me.

But how can an employee at a reindeer farm come up with the money he's bidding?

The prim-and-proper bidder fails to raise his paddle when the reindeer wrangler takes it to one and a half million.

The auctioneer tests the room, inviting bidders who'd dropped out to rejoin.

It finally hits me... I'm getting bid on. Someone will win me tonight. My dream is coming true.

My gaze lingers on the table full of dad potential. They don't spark a fire in my heart the way *he* does. Shifting my attention to the reindeer guy, I realize this was meant to be. We randomly cross paths and he ends up at the auction.

Fate stepped in to make sure I got the guy who can give me what I came here for tonight—an orgasm I'll never forget.

"Sold to the gentleman in the back for one point five million!"

Thunderous applause. My knees wobble. I'm escorted off stage. My heart pounds.

I'm taken to the payment room where I breathe in his woodsy scent. "We meet again."

The muscles in his neck flex. "Because you're mine."

I arch a brow. "You knew I'd be here?"

"Overheard you and Molly at the ranch. Nearly choked when I heard you say you were in the auction."

I remember all too clearly. I remembered everything about him.

The attendant who ushered me to him asks, "Do you accept his win?"

Why the hell wouldn't I? Then my libido relaxes and I recall that we can turn down a winner. The women have agency in this. "Yes, thank you."

The break in my thought pattern is enough to remind me of other things, like my kid. When the attendant walks away, I say, "Look, my life is up in the air right now. I have to get home tonight... you know, the kid thing. So can we do this?"

It sounds terrible when I put it that way, but I'm one phone call away from my night being cut short. Do all moms experience this level of panic and uncertainty?

"You really know how to set the mood." His laugh rumbles between us but his smile is almost nonexistent.

45

I think he's making a joke. I like this playful side of him. "You're the one who broke Christmas Cherry Auction history and didn't come with a group of friends."

"You could have turned me down. I'm sure Mr. Button-Up and his friends would love to try handling a woman like you." The faintest hint of a smile sits on his lips.

"You could have let them win... and watched them try." But I don't want guys who look like they play by the rules. I have that at home, and I love being cared for, but I need more.

I want the guy who shows up in a flannel shirt and drops a million dollars all on his own. I want the guy who can make my heart race from across a corral. I want the guy who makes my sex ache at the mere thought of surrendering control to him.

He shrugs. "It would have been worse than watching you try to untangle yourself from the reins."

I gasp. "I think you liked me being tangled."

He reaches to the back pocket of his jeans and presents small leather reins.

My heart stops. My sex aches and my wrists yearn to be bound again—this time intentionally.

"I wanted you to stay tangled." He sweeps me up, tossing me over his shoulder like I weigh nothing.

His huge strides move us down the hall and into a room. He gently lowers me onto the bed, tosses the restraints beside me, and stares down at me.

Urgency nags at me on many levels. I spread my thighs and he accepts the invitation, letting his gaze linger on my drenched panties.

I reach under my skirt to get rid of them but he catches my hands, shoves them upward and pins my wrists over my head.

The fingers of his other hand tuck into my panties. His expression goes feral. And with one smooth yank, my panties are gone.

I'm seriously impressed, and also glad that I bought the skimpiest pair I could find for this occasion.

Maintaining obsessive eye contact—that's melting me—he brings my panties to his face and sniffs. "I've been craving you since... you were in my arms at the ranch."

"Way to win a girl over—forget where you first saw her. But I forgive you." Was that pause to avoid bringing up the parade incident? Works for me. The only thing that needs to be perfect tonight is my orgasm.

He stuffs my panties in the pocket of his flannel shirt, then together we get the rest of our clothes off. I don't want the dress ripped, as enticingly dramatic as that would be.

He grabs the leather from the bed then catches both of my wrists with one big hand. I nod so fast, I'm not even sure if he paused for consent or if I imagined it.

I can barely take my eyes off of his thick cock to notice the quick but precise movements he binds my wrists with. Wiggling against the leather, I note that he did a specific pattern that allows me flexibility. Nice.

But when he backs me to the bed, I say, "Wait."

He flinches. "Are you okay?"

"Yeah, but if my hands weren't bound, I'd be climbing you right now."

"You want me to undo them?" Disappointment marks his expression.

"No, just bend down so I can get my arms around your head."

"I want to—"

"I've had plenty of orgasms lying in my bed. I want this one to be different." Never mind the fact that it inherently will be since I'm not giving it to myself. But I need this adventure.

He growls, lips crashing against mine. I wiggle my arms up between us, breaking our kiss for a moment to get them over his head.

Following my cue, he cradles one hand under my bottom and lifts me, the massively swollen head of his cock leaving questions about how he'll fit. As impressive as it is, I'm sure he'll fit, and it will hurt less once he's inside of me.

"Are you ready?" he asks, his face pulled beside mine because of my arms.

I take a deep breath and nod. "I'm all yours."

He thrusts in and I cry out. Not wanting him to worry, I say, "Harder. Keep going." Because he set my body on fire. Every nerve ending is lit up. My sex strains around his shaft but it's the most incredible feeling ever.

My breasts flatten against his hard chest and my nipples are stimulated by every movement, every thrust. I wrap my legs around his waist, taking in every bit of him that I can.

An orgasm builds and it's already pure heaven.

We move frantically, him working my body against his. "Ready to be mine forever?"

Flinch. The forever vibe has me touchy. I quickly get back in the groove. Maybe he didn't notice.

Needing to avoid answering, I lose myself in the pistoning of his cock, the pressure against my clit, and I tumble headlong into my orgasm.

My release hits like fireworks, and I go limp in his arms as his shaft swells and he fills me with cum.

His thrusts and growls give way to heavy breaths and we drift through bliss together before he carries me to the bed. We did it!

Carefully removing his cock first and then my arms, he curls beside me, his hand resting on my belly. "We'll be bound forever before the night's over."

Blissy brain loves the command in his voice. But the statement niggles until I realize what he's saying. How to be gentle about this?

"No babies tonight. I have an implant."

A hint of disappointment flashes across his face before he schools it.

As positively as I can, I say, "You did your job. That was incredible."

"But the winners always—"

"I'm sorry." Might as well cut this off with the rest of my story. "It's been less than a week since I was named guardian of my cousin's kid. I haven't had time to process what that means. I won't burden anyone else with that."

He strokes a finger lovingly over my cheek. "Being with you, and whatever else that entails, will never be a burden."

He's saying all the right words. With a little more time, I might be ready to accept them. An idea sparks.

"Could we be friends with benefits for now?"

"Do you say that to all the guys?" His stoic expression makes it hard for me to tell if that's a joke.

"Every single one who's fucked me like that."

Chapter 8

Hudson

I pull into the garage, pop the trunk open, and grab the supplies for our first family movie night. A massive tin of flavored popcorns fits under one arm—Jolene will dive into the cheese, no question, while I claim the caramel.

Mulling spices and a jug of cider are in bags, along with Jolene's favorite store-bought lasagna. I would have made it from scratch but I want my focus to stay on Jolene and Jane—and I'm pretty sure Jolene likes the frozen one as much as mine.

Every kid deserves parents who show up. My goal is to convince Jolene that I'll fill that role with her. This isn't the path I sketched in my head, but it works. I want this family with her.

With one finger, I catch the final bag that contains a toy for Jane. I close the trunk and make my way inside.

A light in the kitchen catches my attention as I deposit the toy bag on the kitchen table. A woman holding a sippy cup—not Jolene—steps into the doorway.

"You must be Mr. Powell."

I freeze, regripping my armfuls. "Who are you?"

"Kendall, the babysitter." She shifts. "Didn't Jolene tell you?"

I ease the load onto the table, one item at a time. The popcorn tin thuds down first, then the cider and lasagna. Proper storage can wait. "Hi, Kendall. No, she didn't mention a sitter. Where'd she go?"

She twists the cup's lid, her gaze sliding away. "I'm not supposed to tell you."

My pulse ticks up. "Why? What if Jane needs something?"

"I know how to get hold of her." Her voice firms, but she won't meet my eyes. "She gave strict orders."

I unclench my jaw. "Do her orders allow me to let you go home? What do I owe you?"

Relief flickers across her face. "Yes, sir, or I can take Jane to my place."

What is Jolene up to? And why doesn't she trust me? Does she think Jane burdens me? It would at least be courteous to let me know a stranger would be in my house.

"How much do I owe you? Jane should stay here."

The toy bag tips to the side and a blanket with different textured tabs along the sides falls out. I catch it, shoving it away from the edge.

"She paid up front." Kendall shrugs and returns the sippy cup to the kitchen. With her purse over her shoulder, she says,

"That's a great pick, by the way. Jane will love playing with those tabs."

"Thanks." It's a small win I wanted to share with Jolene.

Kendall stops at the front door. "Do you want my number in case anything comes up?"

"No, I've got this."

The front latch clicks shut behind her. I pull out my phone and click Jolene's name. It rings through to voicemail but I don't leave one.

I send a text. *I let Kendall go home. Where are you?*

Jolene: *with friends*

Her being out with friends doesn't bother me as much as the clipped answer or her evasiveness.

I preheat the oven and get the lasagna going since it takes a while. I still need to eat even if she doesn't.

The silence in my house sits heavily in contrast to the movie that should be underway.

The evening drags on and I abandon my half-eaten lasagna while staring absentmindedly at an old Sherlock episode that's playing out on the TV. Sherlock would know where Jolene went.

The front door swings open, and while I don't know where she's been, I'm relieved that she's finally home.

She slips in quietly, and I hop up.

Her cheeks are flushed as if she's had quite a night. But contrary to an evening out with friends, she has a couple of her bags that she usually packs for an overnight.

"You're still up." She tries to skirt around me to get to her room.

I touch her arm in a gentle request that she give me a minute. "I am. I was worried."

The musky scent on her devastates me.

"Kendall has great referrals."

"But you didn't tell me."

She shrinks. "Sorry, I was trying to handle everything without burdening you. I'll let you know next time."

"Want some lasagna?"

"Sure, I need a quick shower first." She rushes to her room and I do my best not to think about where she went and what she did. She's home now.

When I hear her padding down the hall, I warm a plate of lasagna. She carries it to the living room, tosses a baby doll out of the chair, then regroups and puts it in the toy bin. She rolls her eyes when she sees Sherlock on the screen.

She may be showered but the scent of another man's cum is burned into my senses. Unable to sit with not knowing, I pry, "Why wasn't Kendall supposed to tell me where you were?"

Jolene stops the fork halfway to her mouth. "It's not like I'll do this every night." She slumps. "I just had to get out."

"I'm not judging."

54

"Then why won't you let it go?"

"There was a stranger in my house."

"I already apologized for that. And I promise, I'm getting a job and I'll move out so you don't have to worry about me and who I bring into your house anymore."

"That's not what I meant. You should go out. You have to take care of yourself. You'll be fresher for Jane if you do."

"I just want you to trust me."

She huffs. "Trust you? Of course I do, you're the nicest, most reliable guy around, which is why I need to get the tornado of my life out of your tidy house."

"I already said you could stay."

"Because you're *too* nice." Her gaze shifts to the new blanket I set on the end table. "Did you get that for her?"

"Yeah." Because I'm the nicest guy around. That's definitely not the stage I want set when I propose to her. I can't have her think I'm doing it to be nice, like I'm saving her from being a single mom. Fuck!

Jolene motions for me to toss it to her. She balances the plate of lasagna precariously on her lap while reaching out. Fighting my love for all things tidy, I risk chaos and toss the blanket.

That's something I've been learning from her, that I can relax a little and the world will still be fine. It's liberating.

Her fingers trail over the tabs—silk, velvet, corduroy. "She'll love this. Thank you." She eats a bite of lasagna then says, "You really are the best brother a girl could have. I should have told you I was getting a sitter. I'll do better next time."

"I truly don't mind taking care of her." Unsure where the line crosses from nice into committed, I say, "I'm here for you. For Jane. We're in this together."

A wail pierces our ears from down the hall. I'm on my feet while Jolene tries to set her plate down and ends up knocking the new blanket into it.

I could have gotten to Jane's room already, but I couldn't stop watching the trainwreck.

"I'll get her." Jolene bolts past me. "You've done enough."

Have I? Picking her plate and blanket up, I stop in the kitchen first, rinse the dish, then take the blanket to the laundry room and spray it with stain remover.

I'm heading to Jane's room when Jolene meets me in the hall and flashes a tired smile. "She'll be up early, I better get to bed."

"Go on. I cleaned your plate."

She pecks my cheek. "You spoil me, big brother."

Stepbrother, I want to insist, but I need a bigger plan than that.

The popcorn tin sits untouched and the cider's cold. Family night crumbled—a real possibility that I'm brother-zoned. I try to laugh at my friend-zone joke, but it's not funny when I have a marriage proposal sitting under the Christmas tree.

All this time I thought I was wooing her, I was doing the exact opposite. How did I get this so wrong?

Is there something to be learned from her fascination with Krampus and her love of monster romances or am I grasping at straws?

I plop onto the couch and pull out my phone, entering a search I never would have imagined doing. Why do women love monster romances?

Chapter 9

Walker

I'm playing a dangerous game with Jolene, risking my heart on a woman who's not ready, as evidenced by how many times she's ignored my calls and given one- or two-word responses to my texts. *Busy* and *I can't* aren't the most encouraging replies.

Plus, I still haven't talked to Jeremy. No easy way to bring up... *Hey, I've felt something for your sister ever since I saw that picture of her. Then I got really turned on when she ended up tangled in the reins... long story. Anyway, I obsessed over restraining her and fucking her senseless, so I bought her at a sex auction and did just that. Now we're friends with benefits.*

Yeah, not something you tell your best friend.

And since I haven't received any irate calls from him, I'm guessing she didn't tell him.

Our phone number exchange at the Aubergine Affair replays in my mind...

After she tormented me by playfully implying she has other friends with benefits, I asked for her number.

When I dialed it so she'd have mine too, I teased her, asking what she was going to list it under since she didn't know my name. It was supposed to give us a playful way for me to tell her without it being weird but she said she'd list me as *Him*.

I would have been happy about a lot of nicknames but that didn't excite me. In fact, the more I thought about it, the worse it seemed.

I should have just told her. If she put two and two together, that Walker who works at the reindeer ranch must be her half-brother's friend Walker who owns the reindeer ranch, then so be it.

But I desperately wanted more time with her. No interference from anyone else like a protective older brother.

Except as I spent even more time trying to figure out how to tell Jeremy, it occurred to me that Jolene might have already figured out who I was. That might have been her motivation behind avoiding my name. Maybe she wants the same thing, more time before we have to admit our relationship would cross a line for her brother.

And all of the dismissed calls and clipped texts truly are just her getting used to taking on a kid.

Enough's enough. Before I confess to Jeremy that I banged his sister, I have to make my feelings crystal clear to her. If she rejects me, we bury the secret forever. But if she'll accept my commitment to her, I'll handle the fallout with her brother.

With a plan in place, and not wanting to let Christmas pass without confessing, I grab my phone.

I type a text, then delete it. I need her voice, and I need to see her as soon as possible.

I dial her number, grumbling that it's going to come up as a call from *Him*. It sounds more like a codeword to know not to answer than a nickname.

To my surprise, she picks up. I shouldn't have gotten in my head about her feelings for me. "You busy?"

"Actually, I'm free." She sounds super relaxed. "Jeremy took Jane to her family's Christmas Eve party."

"That was nice of him." I should probably feel guilty for taking advantage of his kindness, but I don't.

"I offered to go, but he insisted I take a break."

"Are you home alone?" Aside from Jane being gone, I'm not sure if her stepbrother knows she has friends with benefits.

"I am. Do you want me to invite you over?"

"It'll be easier to give you an orgasm if I can put my hands on you instead of this phone."

"Hmmm... I've heard phone sex can be pretty hot. Want to know what I'm wearing?"

"I want your address."

"You are no fun." She laughs then rattles it off.

Slipping the ring box into my jacket pocket, I consider whether I'll give it to her before or after sex. Definitely after. The ring is just a symbol to show my commitment to her, not an official engagement ring because I'm trying like hell to respect her request for time.

Then I grab the bigger gift, her very own set of leather restraints, and head out.

Chapter 10

Jolene

A visit with *Him* is a tease of how I imagined my life would be after the auction... unlimited orgasms from men... well, from *a man* who adores me and didn't give up on me no matter how many calls I ignored or texts I sent short, dismissive responses to.

I crank up Christmas pop songs through the house speakers so it doesn't seem like I'm sitting home alone sulking. The sulking stopped once *He* called.

In my bedroom, I slip into the sexy red lingerie I'd splurged on for after the auction, the sheer babydoll with lace edges. The term 'babydoll' hits me as being awkward for the first time ever. Becoming a mom rewires your brain, turning innocent words into landmines.

I sit at my vanity, open my makeup box and get to work. A swipe of red lipstick, smoky eye shadow, and a bit of body glitter liven me up.

Just because diapers and bedtime stories fill my days doesn't mean I forfeit the need to feel desired.

Jeremy has Jane for the next few hours and Hudson had his mother's family's Christmas party. If not for Hudson's wall calendar, I don't think I could keep all of the Christmas festivities straight. Too many *half* and *step* family celebrations.

The doorbell chimes and I blow my fabulous self a kiss in the mirror before padding to the front door. My heart races and my body yearns for his touch. I'm relieved that he reached out. I'd been afraid that he would give up on me. That's why I didn't want to know his name, less to etch on my heart if he broke it.

It's possible I've misjudged him. Not everyone is as freaked out by suddenly owning a kid as I am. Hudson's certainly risen to the occasion. No time to think about the nicest guy in the world. I need to think about the naughtiest one.

I swing the door open and he's even more stunning in broad daylight. Still in flannel and jeans, but that doesn't much matter since my goal is to get him naked.

What catches me off guard is the gift he's holding.

"I'm so embarrassed," I blurt, crossing my arms over the thin fabric as the cold air tickles my skin. 'I didn't get you anything."

"You didn't know I was coming." His gaze rakes down my body, slow and deliberate.

That warms me right up. I grin, stepping aside to let him in, clicking the door shut behind him.

He pauses to pull me in for a hug. "You're the only gift I ever need."

His embrace makes all of my problems melt away. I should have found time for him sooner, but I can't fault myself for taking a couple weeks to understand my new role. The important thing is that he's here now with no distractions. Except for the ticking clocks of when Hudson will get home and Jeremy will bring Jane back.

Easing away, I toy with the shoulder-tie strap on my lingerie. "Are you going to unwrap me first, or should I tackle that gift?"

He sets the box under the Christmas tree, although he's kind of awkward about it, then turns back to me. "Thought we could hang out, get to know each other, then unwrap things."

"Jeremy's only got Jane for a couple hours."

He adds his fingers to mine at my shoulder. "Then we better get to it."

His tug loosens the bow, allowing the fabric to fall away from my breast. After a sharp inhale, he loosens the other side. The lingerie drifts down my body, leaving me bare since I saw no reason to force him to tear another pair of panties off me.

His hands find my waist, pulling me against him, then lifting me. His mouth claims mine as we step toward the blanket I laid out in front of the tree.

He eases me onto it then stands over me and undresses himself. I always thought booty calls were so odd. Was the other person just supposed to drop everything for sex? Yes, I get it now.

He crawls over me, kissing his way from my foot to my sex, which he deliberately bypasses, same for my breasts, then up to my lips.

His cock presses against my entrance. Now that I know how good it can be, I'm ready to skip all foreplay.

I arch my breasts into him. My leg hooks around his thigh, urging him closer. "Please, I need you."

His growl holds desperation. "I need you too, Jolene. Let's slow down and enjoy this."

"I want to enjoy your cock being inside of me."

He bucks his hips, giving me his tip then pressing further to get past the hardest part. When I breathe again, he stops. "Is that all you wanted?"

I wiggle underneath him. "Are you teasing me?"

He counters with a few small motions that hit just right. "Teasing would be telling you that I had your Christmas present custom made."

I'd swear his cock is custom made for me, but I don't think that's what he means. I try to comment but he plunges inside of me.

"Who do you belong to?" he whispers in my ear.

My heart flutters. My defenses fall away. But how can I be sure this isn't just pillow talk? That one's on me since he wanted to talk first.

"Tell me who you belong to."

Why am I holding back? Why don't I trust him? Why don't I trust Hudson? Oops! Why am I thinking about Hudson? A wild thought rolls through me, imagining the two of them claiming me, fulfilling the promise of the auction.

It unsettles me how much I wish I could have them both. The reindeer wrangler for his take-charge style and Hudson for— I force myself to stop thinking of Hudson while a very satisfying dick is inside of me.

Why now, of all times, does a saying pop into my head... A bird in the hand is worth two in the bush. So what's a cock in the bush worth... I stop my silliness. There's no time for fantasies when I made the choice to have sex under the Christmas tree in clear view of the front door. My bedroom would have offered privacy and less need to watch the clock. As it is, I'm counting on Hudson sticking to his schedule—as Mr. Reliable always does.

"I'm yours." Surrender washes through me as I admit how deeply I want to be with him.

I can't make out what he says because I gasp as he thrusts deep, filling me, his rhythm building fast.

Our bodies intertwine. He rolls me on top of him. His leg bumps into the tree, ornaments jingle, and for a split second we freeze, making sure it's not going to topple onto us.

"You drive me wild," he mutters, his pace unrelenting even from below.

Sweat slicks our bodies, the pop music playing in the background. In this exact moment, my life is perfect. I cry out, shattering around him, and he follows, rolling us back so he's on top.

We lie there, tangled on the floor, eventually rolling onto our sides, tree lights casting colorful patterns across his body.

"We have time for another round." I can't let this opportunity go to waste.

"I unwrapped my present. I think it's time you open yours." He fishes the gift out from under the tree, and I don't question why he'd rather swap presents than cum.

I prop myself on an elbow and tear the wrapping paper off. From my awkward position, I fumble the plain white box while trying to open it. He grabs it, opens the lid, and shows me...black leather cuffs lined with soft fur and studded with silver stars.

I sit up, stunned by the custom design. How did he know I love stars? "Handcuffs? They're so beautiful."

But why are there four?

"Ankles too."

Heat rushes through me. I'm giddy. "And the stars?"

"Seemed perfect for you."

"They are."

"I know you love your freedom, but you also seem to love restraints."

I wrap one of the cuffs around my wrist. "You want to tie me up and fuck me, and you're worried it'll cramp my style? Let me assure you—it won't be a problem."

He gets that feral look again and fastens the buckle on the cuff I tried on.

He leans me onto my back and fastens the other end on the foot of the couch.

I test the cuff—firm, unyielding. He scoots me to the side so my head is between the two couches and he fastens my other arm to the second couch.

The vulnerability hits differently, exposed like this, but it ignites something raw. His hands roam over my entire body, teasing until I'm writhing and tugging at the restraints.

I'm at his mercy, surrendering control to him. Escaping responsibilities. Embracing my sexuality as he explores every inch of me with licks and kisses.

I have a sensitive spot behind my knee that I didn't know about. My stomach does somersaults as he kisses over my belly. My nipples are rock-hard and then some as he teases with his tongue. And my fingers. I had no idea how much I would like him sucking on my fingers.

This is what I dreamed of and it's mine. All I have to do is trust that he wants me. That shouldn't be so difficult.

Then he lines his body up with mine and slides his cock inside. We feel so right together. I'm his, and I mean it.

Ecstasy builds, coiling until it can't be contained any longer. I fracture into a million pieces. I'm glitter floating on the breeze. And I'm his.

He rides through my release, giving me a chance to catch my breath before his cock swells, pushing me right into another orgasm with him.

I hug his body against mine, shocked by how free I feel with him. A million questions should be flooding my brain but there's only one I can't shake... Hudson being a part of this.

Have I fantasized about my stepbrother so many times, I can't accept reality? Guilt niggles at me for where my mind wanders while in these strong arms. I should be happy. I am. I'm more than happy.

Yet, my mind morphs Hudson's kind actions into those of a loving husband. Why can't I just be happy, brain? Should I have snuck into his bedroom one of the many times I heard him masturbating? Could this have all been solved long ago?

My wrangler unfastens my wrists and helps me bring each arm to my side. All of the tugging gave me quite a workout.

He curls behind me, drapes an arm over me, and we listen to the Christmas music while watching the twinkling lights. It's time I grow up and learn to be happy with what I have.

He runs his fingers through my hair, then picks up a strand of tinsel. "Thank you for letting me come over."

I nestle closer, tracing my finger up and down his forearm.

"You can't leave yet, we have at least an hour."

"I'm not going anywhere. I'm just glad this worked out."

"You think I'd turn you down after what you did to me at the club?"

"After what *you* did *to me*, yes, I thought you might ghost me."

"What did I do?"

"Friends with benefits..."

"I did say that. What if we upgrade? I'm not so... nervous now."

He holds me tighter. "Would this upgrade happen to involve a little commitment? No seeing anyone else?"

I laugh. "I don't have time."

"But do you want to?"

"No." I squeeze my hand on top of his. I don't know much about him, but I don't want to lose him. "This is perfect."

"I'm going to get us a drink, then I've got another present for you."

"Another one?" I watch him head to the kitchen, enjoying the flex of his butt muscles—those sexy indentions.

Alone, I roll over, spotting another gift. Different paper, but it's smaller than the first box so I must not have noticed it.

Tearing into the package, I lift the lid and pull out a rolled-up paper.

He calls from the kitchen, laughter in his voice. "Guess you're not waiting for me. I promise, there's no pressure. I'll respect whatever time you need, it's just a symbol of commitment."

"Cups are beside the sink. Alcohol's in the pantry. Plenty of options in the fridge. Make yourself at home." I'm rattling off the directions as I unroll the paper and study the map.

It's an immaculately hand-drawn grid with roads and buildings. Streets are labeled in neat block letters. *Jolene's Adventure Court* and *Happily Ever After Lane* intersect *Our Shared Path*. A legend in the corner reads: *Scale: Lifetime Commitment. Proposed Route: Marry Me.*

My breath catches. It's so... orderly. Nerdy, even funny, like a planner mapped out his feelings. But this isn't the work of a flannel-wearing reindeer wrangler.

I glance back in the box at the unmistakable shape of a ring box. It's wrapped, but it's still obvious.

My heart pounds. I break out in a cold sweat. I've found a new level of vulnerability. At the bottom of the map key, he wrote: *H + J = 4 Ever*

This is from Hudson.

The reindeer wrangler sits beside me. How did I not hear him? He asks, "What's that?"

"Not your second gift?"

He crawls to the tree and reaches way under to retrieve a small box, very similar in size to the other box in Hudson's gift. "This is mine. What's that?"

I swallow the lump in my throat.

"A marriage proposal from Hudson." I don't mean to say it, but the truth tumbles out.

I think I'm going to be sick. I toss the map and box aside and rush to my bedroom. Splashing water over my face is enough to help me focus. I throw sweats on and return to the living room.

"It's really sweet." His words are nice as he studies the map but he's obviously crushed. "I didn't realize—"

The front door creaks open. Hudson steps in. His eyes widen, shifting from me to the naked man holding his marriage proposal.

"Hudson, I'm sorry. I opened the wrong gift."

"Apparently so." He's never looked so hurt. The stepbrother who's been there for me, taken care of me... I thought he was being overly nice. He was getting ready to propose.

I rush to him. "I get it now. I'm sorry I was so dense."

"You weren't the only one who was dense." Hudson straightens his spine and gets a determined look in his eyes.

My naked *friend with benefits* has grabbed his clothes and dressed. "Look man, I love Jolene, but if you two need time to sort things out..."

I'm trying to process the proclamation of love while I follow Hudson's gaze to the black leather cuffs. Kicking the blanket over them, I start to defend myself, then bite my tongue. The less I say the better since I don't even know *His* name.

The auction was supposed to solve my problems, not create them.

Hudson's stumbling on the proclamation for other reasons. "Love her? How long have you known her?"

I won't let them fight. "It's none of your business."

Hudson's tone is abnormally stern. He stands taller. He has a bigger presence. "You are my business, Jolene. I've loved you for years in so many different ways. Why do you think I asked you to live in my house? Why do I pay all of the bills?"

I fight down the wicked desires that come to life now that I know they both want me. Is it anything more than a selfish fantasy that will hurt the most caring guy in the world?

If there's one thing I've learned about timing, it's that it can really suck.

Hudson grabs my arm and pulls me close. What has gotten into him? The possessiveness in his expression rivals the look only one other man has given me—and I seriously curse myself for not getting his name now.

"I did some research and realized I've been going about this all wrong. You don't read monster romances because you want a nice guy to make slow sweet love to you." He wraps his arms around me.

What's happening? He's rock-hard—his erection at least as big as my wrangler's. I want to say something about making slow, sweet love being a good thing... I assume sometimes I'll want that. But I can't get my mind off of his girth long enough to speak.

He continues, "You want to be ravished, claimed by the beast. The monster... the beast... they're metaphorical."

For all of the surprise bravado, he's still very Hudson with his analysis. Before the auction, I couldn't have been sure, but he's right. I nod, struggling to figure out how to handle having both of them want me.

How did I miss it? The most structured guy alive chasing my whirlwind? Was I too caught up in my own storm? "Is that what you've been trying to say all along? You want to marry me?"

"It was, but right now, I want to fuck you. Finally get my hands on the woman who masturbates far too loudly."

Gulp. The first part was really hot, but now he's calling me out. The only person other than myself who's given me an orgasm laughs.

"Do you want your boy toy to watch, or is it time for him to go home?"

"I'm not just a boy toy." The man who is fabulous to play with holds out the ring box. "I had something for her too."

Hudson's bravado falters. "Popular gift this year."

We all laugh but Hudson shoves the box-holding hand aside and resumes his sexy tone. "Do you want him to stay or go?"

Chapter 11

Hudson

If I hadn't figured out how wrong my approach was, I would be a broken man right now. Instead, the pain of seeing her with another man fuels the beast inside me. I've played it too safe, too nice, too controlled for too long.

But this power—it's wild and freeing. No more Mr. Nice Guy. I'll fight for her.

This guy who just admitted he's in love with her leaves me no time to waste. I channel my primal beast, the one I restrained every night I heard her moans when she was alone in her bedroom.

Knocking her door down and claiming her wouldn't have scared her off, it would have brought her fantasy to life.

Finally revealing myself, I buck my hips, letting her feel what she does to me. "All those times you played with your pussy, you pictured me, didn't you?"

"Yes." Her voice is barely audible.

Fire races through me. I nod toward the other guy. "What's it going to be?"

"I want him to stay."

I study her expression. There's something she's not saying. "And..."

"I want you both to fuck me."

I had it all wrong. I'm not here to shelter Jolene from the storm; she is the storm. I'm the shelter, and just have to stay strong enough to stand up to her so she has a safe place to call home.

In my deep dive into monster romance, I read about sharing a woman. That was the least favorite piece of information I took in, aside from all things tentacle. There are far more kinks I want to explore, but some of my favorites still seem so far-fetched, like having her call me Daddy.

I want to be everything for her. That's what I've been working toward. I don't want someone else to share that.

But she clearly feels something for this guy, and he feels for her. If it's what she wants, my education will continue on my terms. "First, you're all mine, then he can join in."

Stranger words have never exited my mouth.

Adding to the strangeness, at that exact moment, the front door swings open. Jeremy enters with Jane's diaper bag and an armful of presents. Jolene stumbles out of my embrace.

"Whoa. Did I interrupt?" Jeremy's eyes dart from me to Jolene to the other guy. "What the hell are you doing here,

Walker?" He points at Jolene and me. "And why were you two so... close?"

Jolene chokes out, "Walker? Your best friend?" Confusion twists her features.

Super weird. Who'd she think he was?

She asks, "Where's Jane?"

"Asleep in the car."

I clear my throat. "Jeremy, regarding your first question, you interrupted big time."

He drops the gifts and diaper bag on the couch, exhales hard, and looks gut-punched. "How could you?" He fixes his gaze on Walker. "When I told you to talk to Hudson, I didn't mean—"

"This is the first time I've ever seen him." I step forward, shielding Jolene.

Jeremy's fists clench. "Then tell me you two didn't win her at that damn auction."

I cross my arms. "We didn't."

"*You* didn't." Walker's voice is surprisingly soft.

Jeremy squares up with Walker "You bought her virginity?"

Walker nods.

Jolene fills me in on the auction while they argue.

"How could you fuck my little sister, Walker? You know how I feel about guys who fuck and duck."

"That's not what this is." Walker's jaw ticks. "I have a ring."

He flips open the box, the diamonds glinting under the Christmas lights.

Jeremy stares, speechless.

I won't let him steal the spotlight. "And so do I." I nod at the velvet box on the floor, kicked aside in the frenzy.

"Is this some kind of joke?" Jeremy asks.

Jolene shakes her head. "No joke. It's my dream. Both of them."

He gapes at her like she's speaking in tongues.

My balls ache, my patience is fraying. "Like I said, Jeremy, you're interrupting. We'll hash this out later." I jerk my chin toward the door.

Jolene asks, "Can you please keep Jane for another hour or so, but call or knock before you come in next time."

He hesitates. "I'm not ever coming in this house without knocking again. Won't even glance in a window." He grimaces, shakes his head, and is out the door.

I yank Jolene back against me. "Now, where were we?"

She grins wickedly. "You were about to claim me and then share me."

I glance at Walker, who nods as if consenting to waiting, despite his pants being tented.

Jolene's fingers hook the bottom of my shirt, peeling it off, then trailing her fingers over my chest and abs before removing the rest of my clothes. I strip her slowly, savoring every inch of the body that I feared was off limits.

She sinks to her knees, eyes upturned and hungry. Not where I thought we'd start.

"Open," I growl.

Her lips part, tongue flicking out as she takes me in. I don't want to know how she got so good at this. I'll assume she's a natural. The vibration as she moans rips a groan from my throat. She bobs, hands gripping my hips, nails digging in. I thread my fingers through her hair, trying to control her.

You can't control the storm.

Too good, too much, too fast. "Fuck, I'm—" I spill down her throat, my fingers working her head on my shaft.

That's not how I wanted my first time with her to go—coming before her, but I'll make up for it.

She swallows around me and slowly pulls off, but my cum trails down her chin. I brush a thumb over it to clean her but she grabs my wrist, guides me into her mouth and sucks it clean.

I laugh, mostly from shock, and lean her down onto the blanket. I spread her thighs, diving in with my tongue lapping her juices from her clit. My fingers plunging deep inside of her.

My cock is already hard again, ready to fill her from this end. She will be marked as mine, but not until I make her come with my mouth first.

She arches, gasps, and when I hit a rhythm, she cries out, her release coating my face, filling my mouth with her sweetness.

Letting her catch her breath, I crawl up her body, my gaze never leaving hers. I slide my aching cock into her. She's so tight, but slicked by her release. I don't allow myself to think about other reasons she might be slick inside, why she tasted a little salty.

We rock in unison as my thrusts grow harder and faster. Her nails rake over my back, marking me as hers. I'll wear the streaks as a badge of honor.

I grind deep, bringing her cries to a fever pitch while I hang on by a thread. Her sweet cunt tightens around me.

"That's right. Come on Daddy's cock." The words are out of my mouth before I realize I've said them. Too many romances. Too many kinks unlocked. Maybe she didn't hear.

Or maybe she liked it. Her body spasms as her climax unfolds, drawing me into euphoria with her. Our combined release spills out with each thrust. Our mingled scents of salty and sweet fill the air.

My head falls beside hers and I hate that I ever have to move.

She teases, "Are you done making a mess of me... Daddy? Can Walker join in?"

I chuckle, rolling off. "I'm a man of my word." No matter how much I channel that inner beast, I'm basically a good guy.

Walker's clothes are gone. He climbs onto her, the two of us maneuvering briefly, making sure Jolene's okay with our positioning.

Walker has her feet on his shoulders. Fine by me since that keeps more of my cum inside. I remain beside her, propping myself on one elbow while my other hand explores her body.

She gasps when he enters her. I can't believe I'm sharing my stepsister—still feeling a little selfish. I lower my mouth onto hers, plunging my tongue between her lips. Kisses are long overdue. I want to plant them over her entire body, but I keep them right there—on her mouth—so she can't see him.

Then I lower my hand to her clit, helping out with her orgasm.

When her kisses falter, I say, "Come for Daddy."

My lips return to hers, swallowing her cries of pleasure and her attempt to answer. She's mine—even if I have to play nice and share.

And as much as I love her calling me Daddy, our family dynamic is already too complicated. I may let that kink go, but she's mine forever.

Epilogue

Jolene

A year later

The sun dips low over the turquoise water. It doesn't surprise me that my mom's getting married again, but she really outdid herself with this Christmas wedding on a tropical island. I've probably been a bridesmaid for my mother more times than most women have been a bridesmaid ever.

And while my family dynamic is a bit chaotic, everyone's pretty accepting of my mom's repeated weddings and my unconventional relationship. Most people probably don't even realize I'm wearing wedding rings on both hands. I plan on stopping at two, unlike my mom.

Jeremy is one of the groomsmen, along with our new stepbrother, Kevin.

I smile proudly as Jane walks down the aisle, tossing flowers along the way, then rushes to sit between Walker and Hudson who are holding our three-month-old twins in the front row. It seems my guys defied the odds and got me pregnant despite the implant.

Turns out, mom life is an amazing adventure. Jane's been one of the best things that ever happened to me. She helped me grow up fast and gives me an outlet to let my inner child shine. I glance to the sky, hoping Jennifer's happy with the life we've given Jane.

One of our other cousins had the answer to why she named me as guardian. Jennifer admired my ability to handle anything that came my way and come out of it with a smile on my face. If anything ever happened to her, she wanted me to share that ability with Jane.

Jennifer may never know how much that vote of confidence meant to me, but it helped me embrace my role in Jane's life.

Mom enters, beautiful as always, and the ceremony is short and sweet. The second it's over the photographer says, "The sunset won't last forever. I need the groomsmen right here for pictures. Bridesmaids, we'll get you in a sec."

Hudson rushes to my side and pulls me away from the wedding party. I guess he found someone else to hold the baby. Based on the mischievous look in his eye, what he has planned isn't for kids. A knot starts forming low in my belly anticipating whatever fun he has planned.

Now that he started reading smutty romance, he's made a checklist of all the things he wants to try. It's as if we've created a monster... the good kind.

We run over the wooden planks crossing the dune, then we duck behind the main building of the resort. The island venue is booked for our private party so no one else is around.

My heartbeat stays elevated even after we stop running. His hands trail over my bare midriff and he reaches for the tie on the back of my bikini top. "Hudson, pictures— What are we doing?"

He understands that my question is about his checklist. "Wedding sex."

"No time to waste." I'm happy to oblige. Who couldn't use an orgasm to help get through a family gathering.

I hike my blue and white flowered sarong and turn to face the building. He takes control of the fabric, tucking the hem into the waistband so it stays out of the way.

I brace my palms against the wooden wall and steady my bare feet in the sand. He shoves my bikini bottom down my thighs and I kick it to the side while he drops his surf shorts to midthigh.

Positioning his cock at my entrance, he eases between my folds. "You're so fucking wet."

"Shut up and fuck me."

Thrusting deep in one smooth motion, his fingers dig into my hips. I gasp, the fullness stretching me in the most delicious way.

He pounds into me... turns out that's almost always the way I like it. I clench my mouth shut in an effort to keep from making too much noise, but as he builds my orgasm one thrust at a time, my moans are hard to control.

Walker's voice cuts through our private moment, low and amused. "I know what you're doing back there."

I glance to the side. He hasn't rounded the corner yet.

Hudson's rhythm falters for a heartbeat, then picks up fiercer. Walker rounds the corner, his broad frame stepping closer, his eyes dark with hunger. He cups my face and claims my mouth in a kiss that melts me.

My body shakes, my knees threaten to give out, and wave after wave of my release ripples through me. Hudson groans quieter than normal, but unmistakable. He fills me with his cum and it drips down my thighs.

Walker wastes no time, barely letting Hudson finish before shoving him out of the way.

"I don't think we have time. They'll need me for pictures."

"Go for it, I'll keep an eye out." Hudson steps to the corner while Walker gets his cock out.

I turn back to the wall, bracing myself, but he grabs one of my arms and spins me to face him.

He drapes his lei around my hand, then brings my other wrist into the circle. Layering the lei on itself, he manages to bind my wrists.

"Ready?" His hands circle my waist and I'm taken back to our first time. But there's no time to reminisce.

I nod and when he lifts me, I circle my bound arms around his head.

He settles me onto his cock, sliding me down until I'm full. He rocks hard as he takes control of my body, pumping me up and down. I cling to his shoulders, balancing, and when the pressure becomes unbearable, I bury my face in my arm.

"Hurry, Jeremy's coming," Hudson warns.

My stifled cries are met with Walker's efforts to keep quiet as we give in to our simultaneous releases. Rushing an orgasm is low on my list of favorite things.

"How close is he?" Walker asks.

"Crossing the dunes now."

Walker steadies me on my feet. "I don't have anything to clean you up."

Hudson grabs my bathing suit bottom and tosses it to me. "Better than nothing."

Jeremy's voice sounds like it comes from just past the corner. "You guys back there? We need Jolene for the pictures."

"She'll be there in a minute."

I barely catch the bathing suit with my bound hands, then drag it between my legs. Walker yanks his suit up then pulls my sarong down so I'm covered. Am I really going to take pictures like this?

Hudson rounds the corner to cut Jeremy off. Walker unbinds my wrists then we follow behind Hudson.

Jeremy's brow furrows as he takes us in and shakes his head. "I really need warning if you plan on bringing our new stepbrother to the mix."

Hudson scoops me up. "I'm not letting her near him. I don't like to share."

Jeremy's confusion carries his gaze to Walker. "But don't you both... never mind, I don't want to know."

He turns on his heels, waving us toward the beach where the photographer waits. Laughter bubbles up from my chest, light and free, as Hudson sets me down and grabs one of my hands. Walker falls in step on the other side, lacing his fingers with mine.

Hudson says, "We should make this a Christmas tradition."

"What? Having sex at your mom's wedding?"

We crack up at the craziness that is our life.

"I was thinking more along the lines of taking a vacation." Hudson kisses the top of my head and Walker does the same, leaving us in a tangle of hugs and kisses.

And we live happily ever after!

Now that Hudson has stopped using restraint, will he put restraints on his to-do list? Walker might be able to teach him a thing or two! This spicy bonus scene is available by signing up for my newsletter.

https://landing.mailerlite.com/webforms/landing/m2x2b9

Bellamie didn't mean to steal Krampus from Jolene. Get the details of her adventure in *Sleigh Bells and Shibari* as part of the Santa Daddies anthology!

https://mybook.to/SDback

More by Sylvie Haas

Sparkles and Spankings

Presents and Praise

Tinsel and Teasing

Holidays and Handcuffs

Wishful and Wanton

Baking and Blindfolds

Carols and Consent

Sugarplums and Submission

Ribbons and Role Play

Eggnog and Edging

Reindeer and Restraints...

Eggplant Canyon Phase 2: The Bratva Moves In

Virgin and the Bratva

Fake Engagement and the Bratva

Secret Baby and the Bratva

Escaping from the Bratva

Stepbrothers in the Bratva

Eggplant County Roller Derby

Rolling with my Bosses

Rolling with my Stepbrothers

Rolling with my Best Friend's Brothers

Rolling with my Fake Fiancés

Rolling with the Single Daddies

Rolling with my Professors

About the Author

Why Choose one hero when you deserve them all!

Sylvie Haas obsesses over dirty-talking heroes who fall hard and fast for the woman of their dreams.

On most days, you can find Sylvie with the wind in her hair, her fingers on the keyboard, and her mind in the gutter as she thinks up new places her characters can get frisky.

Sylvie Haas is the pen name of a USA Today Bestselling author who's been a finalist in multiple romance writing competitions and has been asked to present internationally on writing short stories and novellas.

Sylvie's books are short, age gap, ménage and reverse harem romances, that will satisfy you with a light and fun happily ever after!

www.ingramcontent.com/pod-product-compliance
Lightning Source LLC
Chambersburg PA
CBHW010935120626
46552CB00010B/3264